Astronaut Girl

SILVER AND GOLD

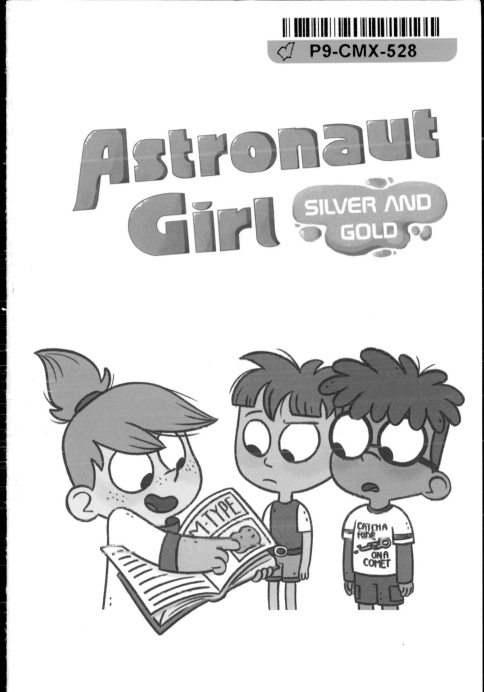

For Renee Kelly, Anu Ohioma,
Jay Emmanuel, and the rest of the
Penguin Workshop team—we couldn't ask
for a better Mission Control!—CH & EV

For Nicola, for being my best friend
no matter how far apart in the
Universe we are—GR

W

PENGUIN WORKSHOP
An Imprint of Penguin Random House LLC, New York

Text copyright © 2021 by Catherine Hapka and Ellen Vandenberg.
Illustrations copyright © 2021 by Penguin Random House LLC.
All rights reserved. Published by Penguin Workshop, an imprint of
Penguin Random House LLC, New York. PENGUIN and
PENGUIN WORKSHOP are trademarks of Penguin Books Ltd, and the
W colophon is a registered trademark of Penguin Random House LLC.
Manufactured in China.

Visit us online at www.penguinrandomhouse.com.

Library of Congress Cataloging-in-Publication Data is available.

ISBN 9780593095775 (paperback)   10 9 8 7 6 5 4 3 2 1
ISBN 9780593095782 (library binding)   10 9 8 7 6 5 4 3 2 1

by Cathy Hapka and
Ellen Vandenberg
illustrated by Gillian Reid

Penguin Workshop

Chapter 1

TOWN FAIR

"I see the top of the Ferris wheel!" I cried. I pointed out the car window. "We're almost to the fair!"

Mom was driving. Daddy turned around from the front seat and tickled my baby brother, who was in his car seat next to me. "Hey, Val," Daddy said. "I bet you can't wait to show Wallace all your favorite things at the fair."

Wallace moved in next door a few weeks

ago. He was supposed to meet me by the petting zoo.

"Daddy, this won't be all fun and games," I said. "Wallace and I still have lots of work to do on our TV script. And the deadline is Monday—that's the day after tomorrow!"

Wallace loved the show *Comet Jumpers*. The show was having a contest for people to send in ideas for future episodes. Wallace and I were doing better than that. We were writing a whole script!

Mom chuckled. "So today will be more of a working playdate, huh?"

"Exactly." I looked out the window again. "Hey, Mom, you just passed the parking lot!"

"Mom is judging the gardening exhibits, remember?" Daddy said. "We get to park in the VIP lot!"

"Cool," I said. Mom is a botanist. That's a scientist who works with plants. She knows everything about vegetables and flowers.

After we parked, Daddy picked up the Baby. I picked up my backpack. It was heavy because my favorite book, *The Universe*, was in there.

Mom waved and hurried off toward the gardening tent. "I'll walk you to the petting zoo and make sure you find Wallace," Daddy told me. "The Baby will want to pet the pigs."

The Baby gurgled. He doesn't understand many words yet, but he knows the word *pig*! He also knows the word *rocket*, since I taught it to him.

The fair was bursting with people, music, animals, bright colors, and interesting smells. Daddy waved to some neighbors as we headed toward the petting zoo. We were almost there when someone called my name. It was Principal Bosko.

"Hello, Val," she said with a smile. "Are you looking forward to school starting on Monday?"

"Of course," I said. "Especially science class."

Principal Bosko started chatting with Daddy. Just then I spotted Wallace. He was leaning over the fence petting a baby goat.

"There's Wallace," I told Daddy.

"Okay, have fun, and you kids stick together," Daddy said. "We'll meet back here at three o'clock."

Wallace was standing with a kid I didn't know. That was a surprise. I thought I knew everyone my age in town.

"Hi, Val," Wallace said. "Carlos came for a visit before school starts. Isn't that great?"

Now I was even more surprised. Carlos was Wallace's friend from his old town. He talked about him a lot.

Carlos grinned. "Yep, it's me, the one and only Carlos!"

Both boys laughed so loudly, it scared away the baby goat. They didn't notice.

Instead, they did a weird, complicated handshake.

"Oh, I almost forgot," Wallace said. "Carlos, this is Val. She lives next door. You can call her Astronaut Girl if you want."

"Is she the one you told me about?" Carlos asked. "The one who's helping you write the script?"

I frowned. "I'm not just *helping him*. We're partners." I turned to Wallace.

"Speaking of the script, we still have a lot to do. We need to figure out a scientifically accurate way for Zixtar to harness the sun's energy to destroy the ice aliens."

Wallace pulled out a homemade action figure. Zixtar was an alien who was the hero of our story. "Zixtar's tentacles can do anything!" Wallace said. "We'll figure it out."

"Okay, but let's eat first," Carlos said. "I'm starving."

I was hungry, too. And every scientist knows that the human brain works better when it's well nourished.

"Fine," I said. "I've been looking forward to my favorite food all year. Follow me."

I led the way to one of the food booths. The boys wanted to stop at the hot-dog stand and the funnel cakes, but I knew what I wanted.

We stopped in front of a green-painted booth. Carlos stared at the sign and made a face. "What's a pickle pop?" he asked.

"It's the best thing ever!" I exclaimed. "It's a pickle-flavored Popsicle!"

Wallace looked intrigued. "I guess I'll try one," he said. "I like pickles."

"Yuck, not me!" Carlos declared. "I'll be right back with my hot dog."

I stared at him. Hadn't he heard me say that pickle pops were my favorite food?

"Don't yuck my yum," I called after him.

Soon we were walking and eating. The rides were up ahead.

"Hey, Val," Wallace said. "Weren't you telling me there's a cool space-themed ride here? What's it called again?"

"Asteroid Attack," I said. "It's my favorite! Let's go on it now before it gets

too crowded."

Wallace ate the last bite of his pop. "Delicious!"

I grinned. "I knew you'd love it! And you'll love Asteroid Attack even more. Come on, let's go!"

Chapter 2

ASTEROID ATTACK!

Halfway to Asteroid Attack, Carlos suddenly stopped short. "Whoa, check out that haunted house!" he cried. "It looks awesome! Let's do that first!"

"I thought we were going on Asteroid Attack," I said.

Wallace looked from Carlos to me and back again. "We did say that," he said. "We can do the haunted house afterward, okay?"

He stuck out his hand. The two of them

did their special handshake again. I rolled my eyes and continued toward the ride.

When we got there, lots of people were in line outside the tent that contained the ride. "There are tons of little kids here," Wallace commented.

"A ton would be two thousand pounds," I said with a laugh. "I don't think there are *that* many little kids here!"

Up ahead, I saw my old babysitter, Tenley, with her baby. One of my

neighbors was holding his twin four-year-olds by their hands.

I waved. "Hi, Mr. Marino. Hi, Tenley."

They both waved back. When I looked at the boys again, they seemed doubtful. "Is this a little kids' ride?" Carlos asked.

"It's for everyone," I said. "Even better, it's scientifically accurate. It's based on the asteroid belt between Jupiter and Mars."

While we waited, I told them more about the asteroid belt. I explained that it's made up of around a million asteroids at least, ranging in size from a dwarf planet down to a pebble. Many contain valuable minerals like gold, silver, and titanium—and some even contain water!

"I wish we could see the ride," Carlos interrupted after a while. "I want to know if it's worth the wait."

"I already told you, it's great," I said. "You'll see."

Finally we made it inside the tent. Now we could see the little red rocket ships moving along the track, letting people on and off.

"There are only two seats per row," Carlos said. "First dibs!"

"Second dibs!" Wallace shouted quickly.

I was confused until they explained. First dibs was a game they played. Whoever called out first dibs got first

choice of whatever they were doing.

"I want to sit in the first row," Carlos said.

"I got second dibs, so I choose to sit there with you," Wallace said with a grin.

I frowned, realizing what that meant. I would be sitting by myself.

I climbed into the seat behind the boys, feeling a little annoyed. But then the music started, and I smiled.

"Here we go!" I cried as the rocket ship moved along the track. "Look, you can see the asteroids now!" I pointed toward the shapes swirling overhead. "There's Ceres! And I think that's Vesta!"

The boys didn't seem to hear me. They kept whispering and laughing. They weren't paying much attention to the ride.

I poked Wallace on the shoulder. "Check it out, right up there is a famous asteroid called Psyche!"

Both boys looked back at me. "Did you

say you want to ride your bikey?" Carlos said.

Wallace laughed. "I likey to ride my bikey!"

Why was Wallace acting so silly? Usually he liked talking about outer space.

When we got off the ride, I asked what they thought. Carlos shrugged. "I bet little kids love it," he said. "As for me, I'd rather go on the Super Laser Space Monster roller coaster at the theme park back home."

"I love that ride!" Wallace exclaimed. "Val, it's awesome!"

They kept talking about all their favorite rides. I didn't say anything. I really thought they'd love Asteroid Attack like I did.

That gave me an idea. "I know something you guys will like," I said. "Follow me!"

Chapter 3

FOOL'S GOLD

I led the way through crowds of
fairgoers to Sideshow Alley. My favorite
game had the biggest sign. It said
"FOOL'S GOLD" in huge sparkly letters.

"This is the best game at the fair," I said. "Look! This year the prize is a gold light stick!"

Carlos laughed. "Are you sure about that?" he said. "Maybe it's an iron pyrite light stick. That's what fool's gold is, you know."

Wallace looked confused. "What are you talking about?"

"Technically, he's right," I said. "I did a school project on this last year. Iron pyrite, which most people call fool's gold, is a mineral that *looks* sort of like gold, but it's really made of iron and sulfur. In the past people used it to start fires, and these days scientists think it could be used to make solar panels." I pulled *The Universe* out of my backpack to show them the page about it.

"Why are you carrying that huge book around?" Carlos asked.

Wallace laughed. "Astronaut Girl never leaves home without *The Universe*."

"We might need it for reference," I told him. "At least, we will if we ever actually get to work on that script!" I looked at Carlos. "How do you know what fool's gold really is?"

"I know a ton about rocks and minerals because my mom works with them. She's a jewelry designer," Carlos said. "Now, how do you play this game?"

I explained how it worked. The game's theme was the California gold rush of the 1800s. Players had to toss a Ping-Pong ball into a shallow pan that looked exactly like the ones prospectors used when panning for gold.

"That looks super easy," Carlos said.

"It's a lot harder than it looks," I warned him. "I'll go first and show you. I've been winning at this game for years."

21

I had just won my first light stick when I heard someone calling my name. It was my friend Ling from school. Our friend Abby was with her.

"Hi, Val," Ling said. "We figured we'd find you here."

"And winning already, of course," Abby added with a grin.

Ling noticed Wallace and Carlos. "Hi, I'm Ling," she said, sticking out her hand to shake like a grown-up. "Who are you?"

"I'm Wallace," Wallace said.

"He's my new neighbor," I told my friends. "That's his friend Carlos. He's just visiting, but Wallace will be in our class when school starts on Monday."

"Awesome!" Ling exclaimed. "On behalf of the student council of Green Leaf Elementary School, welcome!"

Abby laughed. "Don't mind Ling," she told the boys. "She's practicing to run for class president when school starts."

Then she looked at Carlos's belt buckle. It was silver with a large striped brown stone.

"I've never seen a buckle like that," she said. "Did you make it?"

"No, my mom did," Carlos said proudly. "She makes jewelry and other stuff with rocks and minerals. This buckle is made with a kind of quartz called tiger's eye."

"She's an artist? So is Abby," Ling said. "She sculpts really cute animals out of polymer clay."

"Just like Zixtar!" I said.

Wallace showed them his action figure. Abby looked impressed. "Can I see him?" she asked.

She grabbed Zixtar by one tentacle for a

closer look. But then the tentacle broke off!

"Oh no!" Abby cried. "I'm so sorry!"

Wallace took Zixtar back and shrugged. "It's okay. I was thinking about replacing that tentacle anyway."

Carlos glanced at the Fool's Gold booth. "Hey, maybe Zixtar's new tentacle should be solid gold!"

"Actually, that's not a bad idea," I said. "Gold is a very good conductor of heat and electricity, and it doesn't tarnish like copper or silver."

"Cool," Wallace said. "He could totally battle the ice aliens with a gold tentacle!"

"What ice aliens?" Ling asked.

I explained to my friends about the contest and the ice aliens. "The script is due Monday. And this could actually work! Zixtar could use the gold tentacle to harness the sun's power!"

Carlos grinned. "I knew my idea was solid gold! I guess now I'm your cowriter, too."

I frowned. He wasn't a cowriter just because of one tiny idea!

Abby looked at her watch. "Oops, we should go," she told Ling. "We're supposed to meet my big sister in five minutes."

After they left, I returned to playing Fool's Gold. Wallace and Carlos played, too, but their balls kept bouncing out of the pans. I won another light stick.

"Oh, man," Wallace said. "I'm never going to win. Can I have one of your light sticks, Val?"

"No way," I said. "I'm going to make them into a toy for Astro Cat."

"Your cat's name is Astro Cat?" Carlos asked.

Wallace laughed. "I told you, she's Astronaut Girl!"

"Okay," Carlos said. "I give up on this game. Who's ready for the haunted house?"

Chapter 4

THREE'S A CROWD

We stayed at the fair for a few more hours. When it was time to meet Daddy, we went back to the petting zoo. He and the Baby were getting their picture taken with Princess Pinky, the biggest pig in the county.

"Ready to go, Val?" Daddy asked. He smiled at the boys. "Do you two need a ride home?"

"Sure, thanks," Wallace said.

We all piled into the car. Mom was
getting a ride from a friend later because
she was still judging.

"Hey, Wallace, want to go swimming
when we get back to your house?" Carlos
asked.

"No swimming!" I blurted out. "We have
work to do. The contest deadline is the day
after tomorrow!"

Carlos grinned. "Yeah, you'd better write down my solid-gold idea before you forget it."

Wallace balanced Zixtar on his knee. "Too bad your house isn't closer, Carlos. I bet your mom has extra gold in her studio to fix Zixtar's tentacle."

The two of them spent the rest of the ride talking about Carlos's mom's studio and everything else about their old hometown. I couldn't get a word in, even when I tried to change the subject back to our script.

"Here we are!" Daddy said when we got home. "Val, can you take the Baby for a while? I need to start dinner."

"Sure." I picked up the Baby and looked at Wallace. "Where should we work on the script?"

"In your lab, for sure," Wallace said.

"Hey, Carlos, wait until you see this place. It's awesome! Like something at NASA!"

I smiled. "I guess there's enough time for a quick tour," I told Carlos. "Follow me."

We went down to the basement. I could see that Carlos was impressed as he

looked around my lab. He stared up at my scale model of the solar system. Then he pointed at the workbench. "Is that a drone?" he asked.

"Yes," I said. "Daddy and I made it earlier this summer. He's an astrophysicist just like me. That's what you call a scientist who works in outer space."

I was about to tell Carlos more when he spotted Astro Cat sleeping on the 3D printer. "Your cat is cute!" Carlos gave Astro Cat a scratch under his chin. Astro Cat purred. "I think he likes me!"

"All animals love Carlos," Wallace told me. "Hey, Carlos, remember Mrs. Fiddler's dog who hated everyone except you?"

I scowled and shifted the Baby to my other side. Didn't Wallace ever get tired of talking about his old hometown?

Carlos laughed. "Yeah, my poor mom had to make a gold pendant of that dog. Good thing I was there to help!"

Wallace looked at Zixtar. "I wish I was in your mom's studio right now so I could fix this broken tentacle."

"I wish you'd forget your old hometown for two seconds and focus on our script!" I exclaimed at the same time.

WHOOOSH!

Astro Cat squawked as the room began to spin . . .

Chapter 5

THE ASTEROID BELT

"That was wild!" Carlos cried. "I feel like I just rode the most awesome roller coaster ever!"

I looked around. It had happened again! We were on a spacecraft. It was about the size and shape of a school bus, but there was just one big window across the front. The side walls were covered with dials and computer screens. There was a table in front of the window with a couple of joysticks sticking out from the top. A long bench lined the back wall. That was where I was strapped in, along with Wallace, Carlos, Astro Cat, and the Baby.

"Where are we this time?" Wallace wondered.

A computerized voice came from a speaker in the ceiling. "We are currently traversing the main belt."

Carlos looked down at his fancy belt buckle. "Main belt?" he said.

"The main asteroid belt," I explained. "I told you about it at the fair. It's the large group of asteroids located between Jupiter and Mars, just like in Asteroid Attack."

"Speaking of asteroid attacks," Wallace cried, pointing at the window. "Here comes one now!"

I gasped. A huge asteroid was hurtling straight toward us!

It took a second to figure out the release on my seat belt. By then Carlos was already on his feet, running toward the controls.

"I've got this!" he shouted.

"Wait, you don't know what you're doing!" I cried.

"Yes, he does," Wallace said. "He has the top score on every video game at the arcade back home."

"This isn't a video game, this is serious!" I exclaimed.

But Carlos was already using the joysticks to steer. I grabbed the edge of the table to steady myself as the ship lurched to the left. The asteroid loomed bigger and bigger . . . but at the last second the ship skimmed past it safely.

"Whew!" Wallace said. "That was a close one."

Carlos grinned. "Now that's what I call an exciting ride!" he said. "Not like that little-kid ride at the fair."

I glared at him. Before I could respond, Wallace's eyes went wide. "I hope you're ready for another exciting ride," he exclaimed. "Because here comes another one!"

"What?" I cried as Carlos took the controls again. I grabbed *The Universe* and frantically searched through it for the section on asteroids. "Video games and movies make it look like driving through the asteroid belt is like driving a car through a snowstorm. But it's not really like that!" I finally found the right page. "The distance between asteroids is in the range of 620,000 to 1.8 million miles. There's no way we'd see two asteroids so close together unless the ship was targeting them!"

The boys weren't listening. "Farther right, Carlos!" Wallace shouted.

"I'm trying!" Carlos cried.

I stared out the window and gripped
my book so tightly my fingers hurt. The
asteroid was so close that I could see every
detail. It was a smooth, pitted rock like
you'd find in the creek or at the beach,
except it was the size of my house.

"Looks like an S-type asteroid," I said. The
boys weren't listening, but I kept talking,

since facts always calm me down. "There are lots of them in the inner part of the asteroid belt. They're made mainly of iron."

The boys didn't answer. Carlos was leaning way to the right, pulling the joysticks as far as they would go.

"Too close!" Wallace yelled, clinging to

the table. "We're going to hit it!"

The Baby squealed with delight. Astro Cat covered his eyes with his paws.

"I've got it!" Carlos cried, yanking the joysticks even farther. The ship jerked to the right, and the asteroid passed out of sight. Whew! That was close. Astro Cat looked relieved, too.

"You did it, Carlos!" Wallace shouted. "We're clear! That was awesome!"

Carlos let go of the controls. He and Wallace did their weird handshake.

"Just call me Captain Awesome," Carlos said with a grin. "I'm glad I'm here for this instead of some boring moon landing."

"Huh?" I was confused. Wallace and I had visited the moon on our first adventure together. "How do you know about that?"

Wallace shrugged. "I told him all about it. And our trip to the stars, too."

I didn't know what to say. I hadn't told Ling and Abby about any of our adventures. It wouldn't feel right to do that without checking with Wallace. But he hadn't checked with me before telling Carlos.

"Urgent alert!" the computer suddenly barked out. "Large unmapped rubble pile detected ahead. Take evasive measures immediately!"

"No problem," Carlos said, reaching for the controls. "Captain Awesome will steer us through it."

"You can't!" I pointed to the window, where a huge cloud of rubble filled our entire view. "A rubble pile is an asteroid that just got smashed to pieces. The chunks are all shapes and sizes, and

they're all spinning and going crazy.
Even the best video game player in the
world couldn't steer through that without
the ship getting destroyed!"

"Oh no!" Wallace cried. "What are we
going to do?"

Chapter 6

RUBBLE PILE

There was a moment of silence. We stared into the looming rubble pile. Even though some of the chunks looked small, a direct hit from any of them would demolish our ship. What were we going to do?

Suddenly the ship erupted into chaos. The Baby wailed. Astro Cat meowed loudly. Carlos babbled about how if anyone could steer through a rubble pile, he could. Wallace kept waving Zixtar

around and shouting, "Maybe there's an
ejector button!"

Only I stayed quiet. I was Astronaut
Girl, and Astronaut Girl never gives up.
But how was I going to think our way out
of this one?

Even with all the commotion, I heard the computer speak: "Urgent! Manually activate protective force field."

"That's it!" I shouted. "Be quiet, everyone!"

They didn't hear me, because an earsplitting alarm started up. I did my best to ignore the noise as I scanned the controls on each side wall. A computer screen flashed the words *IMPACT 8.9 SECONDS*.

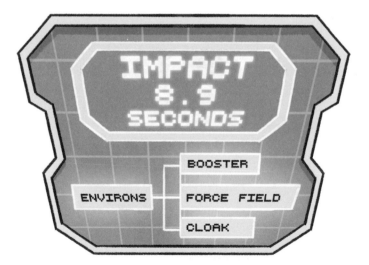

I rushed over. Below the first screen was another that looked like a touch screen. There was a prompt to open the system. When I hit it, a bunch of options appeared. I spotted the words *FORCE FIELD*.

"Got it!" I whispered. I touched the command, then followed the instructions. It wasn't easy, since I was so scared.

The computer spoke again: "Impact in three . . . two . . ."

My hands were shaking when I hit the last command. The alarm stopped. Everyone else quit babbling.

"What's happening?" Wallace wondered.

"Impact averted," the computer said. "Force field activated."

"Cool, thanks for saving us, Mr. Computer," Carlos said.

"You should be thanking *me*," I said.

"*I'm* the one who turned on the force field. While you guys were panicking, I was thinking like a scientist."

The computer spoke again. "Recalculating," it said. "Steering toward the metallic-type asteroid known as Psyche."

"Wait, what?" Wallace said. "*Another* asteroid?"

"Not just any asteroid!" I exclaimed. "Psyche is one of the biggest and best-known asteroids in the main belt! Remember? I told you about it during Asteroid Attack."

The boys stared at me blankly. "You did?" Carlos said.

I sighed. "Yes," I said. I took out *The Universe* and flipped to the page about Psyche. "It's an M-type, which means it's made mostly of metal. The last asteroid

we passed was an S-type, which stands for
silicate or *stony*. The third main type of
asteroid is C-type, for carbon." Suddenly
I realized something. "This must be a
mining ship!" I said. "It's programmed
to locate asteroids for mining minerals.
That's why we keep almost crashing into
all these asteroids!"

Wallace looked interested. "Hey,
computer," he said. "Is Val right?"

There was no response.

"I guess this computer isn't as chatty as the one we met on our trip to the stars," I said. "But we're definitely in the future again. For one thing, this kind of force field technology doesn't exist yet in our time. Plus our scientists are just starting to explore the asteroid belt with robots. We're still a long way from sending people to mine asteroids."

The computer spoke, but it wasn't to answer Wallace's question. "Power usage up ten percent," it said.

"The force field must use a lot of energy," I guessed. "Maybe we should land so the ship can recharge." I laughed, realizing what I'd just said. "Actually, you can't really *land* on an asteroid. You have to join up with it the same way a supply ship does with the International Space Station."

"Really?" Carlos said. "How come?"

I shrugged. "Even a big asteroid like Psyche has hardly any gravity. After all, it's only about the size of Texas." I grabbed *The Universe* again to double-check. "It says here that if you tried to pick up a car on Psyche, it would feel more like picking up a golden retriever."

"Wow, so there's even less gravity than on the moon?" Wallace said. "I bet I could jump like a real superhero on Psyche!"

"You could, but you might fly off into space, since the gravity there wouldn't be enough to bring you back down," I said. "Anyway, we should check it out. It'll be cool to see an asteroid up close."

"No way," Carlos said. "I want to keep

flying around. Steering this thing is a blast!"

Wallace laughed. "Yeah, like a real-life video game!"

I was annoyed. Why didn't they ever listen to me? I'd just saved us all!

But Mom always says you catch more flies with honey than with vinegar. That means you should act nice even when you want to yell at people.

I decided to give it a try. Scientists love experiments, after all.

"Hey," I said cheerfully. "There might be

gold on that asteroid!"

"Gold?" the boys chorused.

I nodded. "Metallic asteroids have all kinds of minerals on them," I said. "It will be our own prospecting adventure."

Mom's advice worked! Now Wallace and Carlos wanted to explore Psyche and look for gold. The ship's controls were computerized, so all we had to do was tell it to anchor on Psyche. We watched through the window as we approached the asteroid, which was irregularly shaped, like a big chunk of rock. Once the computer gave the all clear, I unbuckled Astro Cat and the Baby to let them roam around the ship

"Now what?" Wallace asked.

"There must be space suits on board somewhere," I said. "This looks like a closet."

I opened a door. Hanging inside was a pair of space suits. I realized something. There were only two suits, but there were three of us.

"First dibs!" I shouted.

The boys rushed over. "Second dibs!" Carlos yelled.

"Oh man, you got me!" Wallace exclaimed.

I grinned. "Sorry, Wallace. I guess you'll have to stay behind and watch Astro Cat and the Baby."

Carlos frowned. "No way, he has to come find gold for Zixtar!"

"Fair is fair," Wallace said. "She called it first." He shrugged. "Anyway, Val knows more than anyone about space and asteroids and stuff."

Carlos still looked annoyed. But he nodded. "You're right, fair is fair," he said. "Let's suit up."

Chapter 7

ASTEROID MINING

Carlos grabbed one of the suits. "Whoa, are we exploring an asteroid or going skiing?"

"What do you mean?" I pulled out my suit, too. There was a long pole attached to each sleeve. They *did* look sort of like ski poles.

"What are those for?" Wallace wondered. "Is it really that hard to walk in low gravity? It was easy on the moon."

"The problem isn't walking, it's keeping yourself from floating off into space," I said. "I bet these poles will help anchor us to the ground."

I examined the poles more closely. There were several buttons on the handles. A couple of them controlled a retractable claw that came out of the bottom of each pole.

"I get it," I said. "It's like mountain climbers who have to anchor themselves with each step. We'll have to do the same thing out there. Otherwise, even the slightest jump or misstep could send us flying off into space."

Carlos and I put on the space suits, and I showed him how to work the claws.

"Got it," Carlos said. He stepped out of the ship first.

"Don't forget to anchor yourself!" I called.

"I know, I know," he said. His voice was super loud through the radios in our helmets.

He poked one of his poles into the ground and released the claw. Then he took a step and poked in the second one.

"Which button releases the claw on the first pole?" he called. "Oh wait, it must be this one."

Suddenly he floated up into the air, even though his poles were still in the ground!

"No, you can't let go, or you'll float away!" I yelled. "Hang on, Carlos, I'll save you!"

I slammed my pole into the ground and leaped up as far as I could without letting go. But it wasn't far enough. Carlos was floating above my head.

"Whee, I'm flying!" Carlos exclaimed. He laughed.

I wasn't laughing. I felt more like crying. I was in charge of this mission. What kind of captain would I be if I let one of my crew float off into space? What would Wallace say?

"Don't panic, Val," I muttered to myself. I had to save Carlos before he became a satellite. Daddy would tell me to observe, plan, and react.

So I looked carefully at Carlos. That's when I noticed something. He was still holding the handles of his poles. Bright orange cords ran down from the handles to the main parts of the poles, which were still anchored in the ground!

"Carlos!" I said, letting out a huge sigh of relief. "I think you hit the wrong button."

I was right. We figured out that two of the buttons on our poles controlled retractable tethers, sort of like dog leashes That meant we could move around without using the poles for every single step.

"This is so cool," Carlos exclaimed. "Watch me dunk a basketball!"

He hit the button again and flew up, pretending to dunk. I sighed.

"Let's get to work," I said.

He didn't answer. He was doing a bunch of cartwheels and laughing loudly. He disappeared behind a huge, jagged rock.

It was a good thing we were in low gravity because I had a lot to carry.

Luckily, the space suit had a built-in backpack. My space pack was in there, plus some hand tools and other equipment from the ship. Once we found a good vein of minerals, we could activate the ship's mining robots to dig it out.

I caught up to Carlos behind the giant rock. He was doing a handstand.

"Yowza!" he cried. "I bet I could beat the long jump world record up here!"

He started jumping as far as his tether would let him. I glanced around.

"This looks like a good spot to dig for minerals," I said.

I anchored both my poles and grabbed a pickax out of my backpack. I also pulled out a large, sturdy sample bag that had its own pole to anchor it in the ground. The surface of the asteroid was reddish colored, and dust flew up and floated away when I hit it with the pickax.

"You can use the shovel if you want," I told Carlos.

He didn't answer. Now he was doing one-armed push-ups.  It made me wish Wallace had called second dibs. At least then I'd have some help!

Digging was hard work. I used the pickax, a drill, and a shovel. Whenever I found something that looked like a mineral, I put it in the sample bag.

Finally I stopped to rest and see what I'd found so far. I pulled a chunk of rock out of the bag. It was pinkish orange and kind of soft.

"Hey, I think this is copper," I told Carlos.

"Oh, I know all about copper." Carlos stopped jumping around. "Mom told me it was one of the first metals that people ever used to make stuff. She gets tons of orders for copper bracelets and rings."

"Copper isn't only good for jewelry," I told him. "It's one of the minerals you need for a healthy diet."

"Sounds tastier than a pickle pop, too," Carlos said with a laugh. He started hopping in place, going higher each time. "But forget copper, we're here to find gold for Zixtar's tentacle."

"Maybe his tentacle could be copper instead," I said. "It's easy to work into the right shape. Plus it's even more conductive than gold."

"No way—Zixtar deserves the best," Carlos said. "Copper isn't a precious metal like gold or platinum. Even something like silver or cobalt would be better than copper."

I was glad to hear he was open to other ideas. Sure, gold is good for all kinds of stuff. It conducts heat and electricity. It also reflects better than most materials—that's why the visors on astronauts' helmets are coated with gold to reduce glare and heat.

But other metals are conductive, too, and any of them could work with our script. I started telling Carlos about some of them as I went back to digging. I wasn't sure if he was listening. He kept switching between handstands and cartwheels.

I dug out a shiny, silvery chunk. Silver would work for Zixtar's tentacle! But how could I identify it for sure?

Silver is a soft metal, so I picked up a trowel and poked the silvery rock. It didn't give at all. That meant it definitely wasn't silver . . .

"Carlos!" I exclaimed. "I think I just found rhodium! That's the rarest mineral there is!"

I grabbed *The Universe* out of my pack to look up more about rhodium. It was pretty interesting, so I read it out loud. Rhodium is used in microscope lenses, medical equipment, and all kinds of other important stuff.

Carlos was still in a handstand. But he wasn't moving. I realized he *was* listening!

"Wow," he said. "Now I see why you drag that book around. No wonder Wallace is always talking about how smart you are."

"Thanks," I said, surprised. "Do you think Wallace might like to use rhodium for that tentacle?"

"I'm not sure," Carlos said. "But he should see this. I'll go in and give him my space suit."

"Are you sure?" I was surprised again, since Carlos was having so much fun with the low gravity.

"Sure. Stay here while I send him out." He smiled at me through his helmet. "He'll need Astronaut Girl to explain it to him."

Chapter 8

A SOLID-GOLD IDEA

I reminded Carlos to show Wallace how the tether poles worked. Then he bounced off and disappeared around the big rock. While I waited for Wallace, I looked for more rhodium. I dropped another small, silvery chunk into

the bag just as my helmet radio crackled to life.

"Val, where are you?"

It was Wallace. I told him to come around the big rock. A second later he bounded over and saluted me with one of his poles. Luckily, the second one was anchored safely in the ground.

"Carlos told me about the rhodium," he said.

That reminded me how surprised I was when Carlos offered to trade places with Wallace. Before that, I thought Carlos only cared about silly stuff like video games and haunted houses and doing handstands.

"Carlos is nicer than I thought at first," I said.

"He *is* nice," Wallace said. "I was afraid

you guys didn't like each other, which was weird, since you're both my friends." He smiled at me through his helmet. "That reminds me of a song Great-Grandma Ruby taught me. It goes, *Make new friends, but keep the old. One is silver and the other, gold.*"

I smiled back. "Speaking of silver and gold and other metals," I said, "let me show you where I found the rhodium. Maybe we can dig out enough to make Zixtar's tentacle."

Wallace grabbed a pickax in one hand and a chisel in the other. "Show me where to dig," he said.

We went to work side by side. While we dug, I told him all about rhodium. He listened carefully. When I finished, he looked uncertain.

"Rhodium sounds cool," he said. "But I still really like the idea of a gold tentacle. Did you find any gold?"

"Not yet," I said. "Why are you so stuck on gold?"

Wallace grabbed his notebook out of his space-suit pocket and held it up. That was where he wrote all his story ideas.

"While I was in the ship looking for snacks for the Baby, I was thinking about our script," he said. "What if the ice aliens think Zixtar's new tentacle is fool's gold that isn't strong enough to conduct the sun's rays—but it's actually *real* gold? So Zixtar tricks them and triumphs!"

"That would be a great twist ending,"
I agreed. "It's scientifically accurate, too.
We should use that in the script even if we
don't find any gold for the real tentacle."

"Okay, but let's keep digging," he said.
"You never know."

We went back to work. I was still
thinking about Wallace's script idea. It
would work great. But I could tell Wallace
really wanted to make a tentacle to match
the idea. How could we do that if we didn't
find any gold? Was there any other way to
make it work?

"Check it out!" Wallace cried suddenly.
"I found something!"

"Is it gold?" I moved closer to look.

He grinned. "Only if gold comes in
blue," he joked. "No, I think it might be
cobalt!"

I was excited. Cobalt is a really interesting element. It's naturally magnetic, and can be used to color blue paint, ink, and glass.

"Hey, wait a minute," I said. "How did you recognize cobalt?"

"Carlos's mom uses it to make jewelry," Wallace said.

"Maybe I should let Carlos take my space suit and come out here," I suggested. "He could probably identify the cobalt more accurately than we can."

I couldn't wait to hear what Carlos thought of our cobalt discovery. Maybe he wasn't a scientist, but he knew his minerals. I could be friends with someone like that.

When I rounded the big rock, I stopped in shock. The ship was gone!

Chapter 9

COLLISION COURSE

"Wallace!" I shouted. "The ship is gone!"

Wallace raced around the rock. He gasped. "Where did it go?"

"Carlos better not have taken off without us," I said. "This isn't a video game!"

Wallace looked worried. "He wouldn't just take off and leave us here," he said. "Are you sure it was right here?"

He released his tether and rushed forward.

CLUNK!

"Ow!" Wallace cried, falling back. "There's something here! And it's hard!"

I anchored my poles, then stepped forward carefully with my hands stretched out. After a second I felt something large and solid.

"I think this is the ship," I said, amazed. "It must have some kind of cloaking device."

Wallace gasped. "Just like in episode seventy-six of *Comet Jumpers*!" he exclaimed. "Commander Neutron used a cloaking device to sneak into enemy territory on the electric slug planet. It made his ship totally invisible! Carlos must have turned it on."

"Wow," I said. "Future technology is amazing! I bet it's done with light waves." Then I gulped. "Wait! If we can touch the

ship, the force field must be off. Any stray asteroid could crash into the ship and damage it!"

We felt our way along the ship until we found the door. When we opened it, loud polka music poured out. Carlos and Astro Cat were dancing, while the Baby clapped along.

"Hey, guys, you're just in time for Captain Awesome's dance party!" Carlos exclaimed.

I rushed to the controls. Sure enough, the force field was off. I turned it back on.

"What are you doing?" Carlos asked.

"Did you turn off the force field?" Wallace asked him.

"Not on purpose," Carlos said. "The Baby was getting fussy, so I flipped a few switches looking for some music. That always helps my little cousins settle down. No biggie."

I could tell he had no idea what he'd done—or the danger he'd put us in. Even a pebble-size asteroid could have punctured the shell of the ship! Then how would we get home?

Before I could explain that, the computer beeped loudly. "Energy level dropping. Now at fifteen percent."

"Yikes," I said. "The cloaking device that Captain Not-So-Awesome turned on must be using a ton of energy." I studied the controls until I figured out how to turn it off.

"Hey, Carlos," Wallace said. "Val said you can use her suit to go back out."

"Not so fast," I warned. "Fifteen percent isn't much energy. Maybe we should head home before we run out completely."

"No way!" Wallace protested. "We didn't find any gold! And I still need to show Carlos that cobalt!"

A loud alarm suddenly blared, and red lights flashed everywhere.

"What's going on?" Carlos cried.

The Baby gurgled and pointed happily at the window. I turned to look and froze in terror.

"There's a huge asteroid coming

straight for us!" I cried. "Even the force field might not be able to handle something that big. We need to get out of here—now!"

"Wait!" Wallace said. "The mineral bag is still out there! I'll just run out real quick and grab it."

"There's no time! It's going to be a direct hit," I said grimly. "Buckle in; I'm initiating takeoff protocol."

The boys stared at the oncoming asteroid. It looked bigger already. They didn't argue anymore. Wallace grabbed the Baby, and Carlos grabbed Astro Cat. Soon all four of them were strapped in.

I finished the launch sequence and joined them. "Hold on, everyone!" I cried. "I hope we still have enough energy to make it home."

"I'm sorry—it's my fault we're low on energy," Carlos said. "I ruined our adventure."

"You didn't ruin anything," I told him. "Anyway, we could save a little energy by steering manually once we're away from the asteroid. You should do it, since you're such a good pilot."

He smiled. "You're not so bad, Astronaut Girl."

"You're not so bad yourself, Captain Awesome," I said. "Or maybe we should call you Mineral Boy."

We all laughed. Wallace looked happy as he sat between us.

"Who ever said three's a crowd?" he joked.

Chapter 10

SILVER AND GOLD

A few minutes later, Carlos was steering us through the asteroid belt. It was a beautiful ride, but the Baby didn't seem impressed. He was still fussy. He loves to play peek-a-boo, so I played with him.

"Peek-a-boo!" I cried.

I covered my eyes. When I uncovered them, we were back in my lab in the basement.

"Hey, we're home!" Wallace said.

"Aw, already?" Carlos sounded disappointed. "That was the best ride ever!"

Wallace pulled out Zixtar. "Plus it gave us a great idea for a twist ending for the script."

We told Carlos about Wallace's idea to trick the aliens into thinking the gold tentacle was made of fool's gold. Carlos thought it was great, too.

Then Wallace frowned. "I just wish we'd found the gold for Zixtar's tentacle."

Carlos nodded. "Maybe I can send you some gold from my mom's studio when I go home tonight."

Wallace smiled. But I could tell he wanted to fix Zixtar right now. How could he do it without gold?

Then I had a great idea. "Fool's Gold!" I blurted out.

"Huh?" Carlos said. "The tentacle has to be *real* gold!"

"No, I mean the game Fool's Gold." I grabbed the gold light sticks I'd won at the fair.

Wallace didn't look convinced.

"Here, Wallace. This is the perfect size to be a tentacle," I said. "He'll look like he has a tentacle made of gold lightning!"

Wallace's eyes lit up. "You're right!"

"Awesome!" Carlos exclaimed.

That gave me another idea. "Here, Carlos, you can have the other light stick." I handed it to him. "Then you'll always remember our asteroid adventure."

"Thanks, Astronaut Girl," Carlos said with a grin. "I have an idea for something else to help us all remember this trip."

He showed us a cool three-way

handshake he'd just invented. It included a whistle, a couple of karate moves, and hopping on one foot. It was much better than their old, two-way handshake. In fact, it was exactly 33.3 percent better!

★ ★ ★

Sunday after dinner, Wallace and I sat in the den at his house. Our *Comet Jumpers* script was on the computer. Carlos's face was looking out at us from one corner of the screen. He was joining us from home on video chat.

"Did you guys attach the script to the email yet?" he asked.

"I'm doing it now." I clicked on the attachment. Then I looked over at Wallace. "Ready to send it?"

He took a deep breath. "Let's press it together," he said. "One, two, three . . ."

We hit the key to send the email to the producers of the show. Carlos cheered and waved his light stick.

"I'm sure you'll win the contest," he said. "I have to go pretty soon. Mom wants me to take a bath to get ready for the first day of school tomorrow."

"Don't remind me," Wallace said. "I'm the new kid this year."

"You'll be fine," Carlos told him. "You already have one great new friend." He grinned at me. "And remember what your great-grandma says about old and new friends. One is silver—"

Wallace smiled, too. "And the other's gold," he finished. He started singing the song Great-Grandma Ruby taught him.

Carlos and I happily sang along.

The boys kept singing it over and over again, but I started thinking more about the song's words.

"You know, the song is actually scientifically accurate," I said. "Old and new friends are both valuable, and so are silver and gold. For instance, they're both excellent conductors of electricity and malleable enough to form any size or shape you need . . ."

By then, the boys were laughing instead of singing. "Spoken like a true Astronaut Girl," Wallace said.

Carlos nodded. "And a true friend."